Cathy

cahcy

This edition published by Parragon Books Ltd in 2014

Parragon Books Ltd
Chartist House
15–17 Trim Street
Bath BA1 1HA, UK
www.parragon.com

ISBN 978-1-4723-6077-9

Printed in China

PaRragon

Bath • New York • Cologne • Melbourne • Delhi
Hong Kong • Shenzhen • Singapore • Amsterdam

Meet four lucky pets who came to be loved by four princesses. Then enjoy reading their stories.

First, there is Teacup.
This elegant pup is extremely
talented. Teacup performs
for the villagers every day
in the village square, hoping
someone will notice her.
Some days she finds it easy
to shine and is rewarded
with treats.

Next, there is Treasure. This little kitty is sweet, brave and, most of all, curious. Most cats are afraid of water, but not Treasure!

She spends her days on the
beach playing in the waves,
dreaming of adventure …

… and collecting beautiful
trinkets from faraway lands.

Then there is Bayou – the classiest
and most regal pony you will ever meet.
Bayou lives in the tiny country of Maldonia,
but she is moving to a big city.

Prince Naveen's parents are taking Bayou across the ocean to New Orleans.

Although Bayou is scared about moving, she bravely boards the ship and sets sail for America.

Lastly, there is Sultan. He may be a little tiger, but Sultan always tries to be brave. If you can't find Sultan prowling through the jungle protecting his friends, then he is probably guarding the fancy silk fabrics at Agrabah market.

The owners of the market stalls always reward Sultan for his bravery. But what Sultan wants more than anything is a home of his own to protect.

At the moment, the little tiger sleeps in a roll of fine silks – but that is all about to change.

One bright morning, Belle is walking through the village. She stops to watch Teacup perform her signature move. Just then, sunlight catches one of Belle's earrings, blinding the little puppy.

The teacup on top of her
head wobbles, then it falls to
the ground and breaks. The
villagers shake their heads and
walk away. But Belle doesn't
want to leave Teacup all alone.

Princesses always look after a friend in need.
When all the villagers have gone, Belle kneels
down and picks up the broken pieces of the teacup.
"Don't worry, sweet little pup. I'll help you,"
says Belle. Then she carries Teacup home.

At Belle's palace, the pup is presented with her teacup, perfectly repaired.

Teacup had dreamed of being noticed. Now, she is Belle's little star, performing just for the princess … unless she's performing in the village square, where she always wears sunglasses!

One day Treasure is feeling curious
about the sea, so she stows away on a ship.
Little does she know that this ship belongs
to Prince Eric!

Imagine the royal
crew's surprise when
they discover the furry
little stowaway!

Treasure worries the crew
will make her scrub the decks
or walk the plank.

But no, Prince Eric wants to adopt Treasure! The kitten
with the shiny red hair reminds him of someone he loves
very much. And that special someone is boarding the
ship today. All hands – and paws – on deck!

As soon as Ariel sees Treasure, the princess falls in love with the sweet little kitten. Ariel picks up Treasure and cuddles her close – she smells of the sea, which makes Ariel very happy. Treasure purrs softly in the princess's arms.

When the ship returns to port, Treasure follows Ariel to her palace.

Treasure is now Ariel's little treasure!
They spend their days on the beach,
collecting trinkets, swimming together
and having exciting adventures.

After a long ocean voyage, Bayou finally meets Princess Tiana. Bayou has arrived just in time for the Mardi Gras Parade and the princess has a surprise for her new pony – a costume!

But Bayou isn't used to colourful costumes. She feels like she's a long way from home.

Luckily, Tiana has just the thing for her new pet – a slice of homemade apple pie.

Bayou starts to feel better and when she hears the parade music, the little pony starts to prance!

Tiana is so happy to see Bayou enjoying the parade. The little pony is having such a good time that Tiana thinks Bayou should join the party. The princess arranges for Bayou to take centre stage on one of the parade floats!

Bayou now adores New Orleans,
parades and dressing up. But she adores
her best friend, Princess Tiana, even more!

One day, Princess Jasmine is wandering through the market, enjoying the scent of colourful spices and freshly-cut flowers. She spots a pile of fine silks. Jasmine touches the smooth fabric and imagines a beautiful new dress. Suddenly, her hand brushes something fluffy ...

... and a little tiger appears!
Sultan is confused –
he doesn't feel very
brave anymore. But there's
nothing to be scared of.

Jasmine thinks the little tiger is the cutest
thing she's ever seen! She forgets all about
the silks, her eyes are fixed on Sultan.

Jasmine asks the merchant if she can take Sultan home with her. Although he will miss the little tiger, the merchant knows the princess will take good care of Sultan.

On the way home, Jasmine tells Sultan all about her palace.

That's when Sultan realizes his dream of
having a home of his own is about to come true!
Sultan might be a little tiger but, like all
palace pets, he protects his beautiful new home
– and his princess!

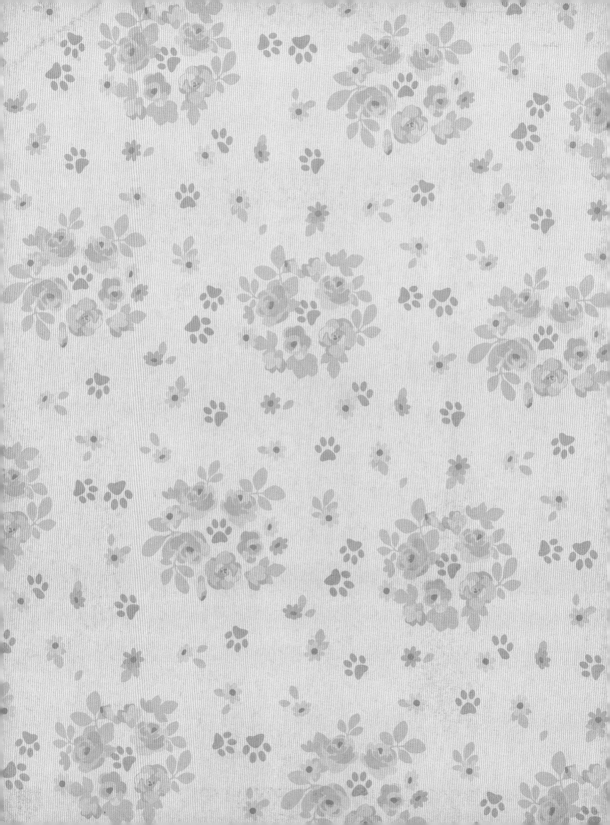